For Cleo Sylvestre, the *real* Honey.

Gaspard Best in Show
Published in Great Britain in 2019 by Graffeg Limited.

ISBN 9781912654673

Written by Zeb Soanes copyright © 2019.
Illustrated by James Mayhew copyright © 2019.
Designed and produced by Graffeg Limited
copyright © 2019.

Graffeg Limited, 24 Stradey Park Business Centre,
Mwrwg Road, Llangennech, Llanelli,
Carmarthenshire SA14 8YP Wales UK
Tel 01554 824000 www.graffeg.com

Zeb Soanes and James Mayhew are hereby identified
as the authors of this work in accordance with section
77 of the Copyrights, Designs and Patents Act 1988.

A CIP Catalogue record for this book is
available from the British Library.

eBook ISBN 9781912654680 from Amazon, Apple (iTunes
and iBooks), Barnes & Noble, e-Sentral, Google Play,
Kobo, Overdrive.

Audio Book available on Audible, Amazon, and iTunes.

123456789

Gaspard Best in Show

Zeb Soanes & James Mayhew

This book belongs to:

_____

_____

_____

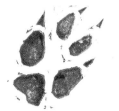

GRAFFEG

Peter the cat was lying on a bundle of old clothes, listening to the radio. He saw a smudge of orange dart between the parked cars. It was Gaspard.

2

'Isn't it glorious?' said Gaspard, looking up at the clear blue sky.

Peter was unmoved. 'There are showers in Hebrides and visibility is poor.'

'Oh dear,' said Gaspard. 'How do you know that?'

'I've been listening to the *Shipping Forecast*,' replied Peter.

Gaspard glanced down the road. 'I'm looking for Finty,' he explained. 'I want you to meet her.' Finty was Gaspard's new friend, a little dog with curly brown hair.

Peter raised his nose. 'Dogs are extremely vulgar – they're forever sniffing unmentionable parts of each other's anatomies.'

Gaspard was shocked. 'I'm sure Finty doesn't do that, she's brilliant.'

'Besides,' continued Peter, 'it's not safe for you to be out in broad daylight. A gardener round here hired a man to get rid of the likes of you for digging up his flowerbeds. I thought foxes were supposed to be *crepuscular*?'

Gaspard looked puzzled.

'It means,' continued Peter, feeling extremely clever, 'you only go out when it gets dark.'

'Then come *with* me,' begged Gaspard. 'You can keep a lookout.'
'Sort of a *guard cat*,' thought Peter, and it made him feel important.

'Where does it live, this dog of yours?'

'That's just it,' sighed Gaspard, 'I don't know.'

'You've got a nose,' said Peter, hopping down to him. 'We'll just have to follow it.'

They set off through the streets, Gaspard keeping his nose to the ground and Peter trotting along the tops of walls, keeping an eager lookout for angry gardeners.

The nose led them to a noisy square, full of people. Gaspard hid
while Peter popped up a tree to get a better look.

'It's the fete,' he called down. 'My owner is running the cake stall and there are a lot of dogs in dressing-up clothes. You'll *never* find her.'

Fancy Dress
* DOG SHOW *

'Why are they wearing clothes?' asked Gaspard.

'It's for the Fancy Dress Dog Show,' explained Peter. 'They do it every year. It's ludicrous.'

'We have to get closer,' said Gaspard. 'She *must* be there.'

They crept along until they came to a saggy old bouncy castle where people were waiting with their dogs. One barked loudly and Gaspard hid under the nearest table.

It was the clothes stall. When he appeared again Gaspard had his legs tangled in a frilly shirt and a pair of satin shorts caught over his ears, like a floppy hat. This amused Peter.

'You look like one of the *Musketeers*!' he observed. 'They were the finest swordsmen in France.'

A voice bellowed, 'Whose dog is this?!' and
before either of them could run away, a stout
woman in green wellies grabbed Gaspard
by the neck and led him to where the
other dogs were waiting.

Peter sprang up onto the cake stall, where he could see everything, next to a large plate of éclairs.

There, among the dogs, dressed as a pirate, was Finty, with a toy parrot attached to her collar.

'What are you doing?!' she whispered anxiously to Gaspard. 'You'll get caught! And what *are* you wearing?!'

'Peter said I looked like a musketeer,' said Gaspard. 'I've brought him to meet you.'

Peter bowed to Finty and purred, 'Charmed.'

Finty looked up and at that very moment a little pug sniffed her bottom.

'SEE!' Peter exclaimed triumphantly. 'I told you what they get up to, it's OUTRAGEOUS!'

Gaspard looked at Finty.

'What?!' she replied. 'It's the doggy handshake.'

A beagle next to them snorted at Gaspard.
'What are *you*?'
'A musketeer?' answered Gaspard weakly.
'What *dog*?' the beagle growled.
'A rare Japanese breed,' interrupted Finty, '*very* expensive.'
'Don't like 'em,' snarled the beagle. 'Too much like foxes.'

A confident voice announced, 'Ladies and gentlemen, boys and girls, WELCOME to the Dog Show!'

'That's my owner, Honey,' said Finty. 'She's famous – she's been in films and everything.'

Finty ran to Honey, who lifted her up, introducing her to the crowd. 'And this is my dear Finty, or should I say *Pirate* Finty!'

Honey led Finty around the display ring. Everybody clapped politely.

Peter pulled a bored face as he helped himself to a large blob of cream from an éclair.

Next, a spaniel dressed as a cowboy ran around the ring. Its owner shouted 'BANG!' The dog rolled over and played dead. Everyone went wild, whistling and cheering. 'Show-off!' muttered Peter, licking cream from his paws.

'You're next,' whispered Finty. 'You'll have to *do* something.'
A little boy had dropped a toy sword on the grass. Finty picked it up with her teeth and passed it to Gaspard.

As he stepped out, the beagle placed a strong paw on Gaspard's tail, pulling him up onto his back legs. Everyone gasped!

The beagle let go and Gaspard tottered forward, waving his sword
in his jaws, just like a real musketeer, to keep his balance. Everybody
cheered and Gaspard managed to walk all around. People stood up,
clapping.

'I think we have a winner!' shouted Honey and winked at Gaspard as she slapped a shiny rainbow rosette on his hat, which slipped down and covered his eyes.

He wobbled to the left...

and to the right...

...and then, with gathering speed, CRASHED into the bouncy castle, plunging his sword deep into a turret.

For a moment, everything was still.

Then a high-pitched noise pierced the square, making the dogs bark and everyone cover their ears.

Gaspard kept tight hold of the sword and with a terrible *THRRRRRUUUUUPPHHHH* it tore a great *hole*!

Air WHOOSHED out, blowing his costume high into the air.

'It's a FOX!' cried a mother.
'*Knew it!*' snarled the beagle, dragging its owner across the square.
'RUN!' barked Finty.

There was chaos. Gaspard raced through the crowd, dived under the cake stall and out of the square, toppling cups and plates everywhere. Peter was thrown into the air, landing... *SPLAFFFT!* ...on top of the éclairs.

'The INDIGNITY!' he declared, wiping *delicious* cream off his face.

Afterwards, as Finty walked home with Honey, she spotted
Gaspard hiding behind a bin and gave him an affectionate lick.

'Well, well,' said Honey, 'is this fox a friend of yours?' Finty barked.
Honey looked at him sternly and Gaspard lowered his head.
'You caused quite a rumpus,' Honey continued, 'but I don't care.'

She led them down some steps to her garden flat and opened the door. 'You see...' she said with a twinkle, '...it *takes* an actor to *spot* an actor.'

Behind her, the hallway was filled with posters and photos of all the shows and costumes in which she had performed. 'It doesn't matter *what* you are,' she said, 'you won today because everybody thought you were great.' Finty jumped and barked approvingly.